Motherfucking Wizards

An erotic novella about sexual wiz

The characters in this book are totally fictional and not based on any other characters or anything, because my imagination is more powerful than you can comprehend.

Written in London, Ontario, Canada

First edition (1.1)

Published by Forest City Pulp

@ForestCityPulp

http://www.forestcitypulp.com

Sign up for news and deals: http://eepurl.com/WZPvD

About the Author

Leonard Delaney has been a freelance novelist since 2012. He writes from the heart instead of wasting time with research or experience. His debut publication, Sex Boat (an erotic novella about sex on a boat), earned him several dollars in royalty payments. Living a clean lifestyle has allowed Leonard to focus on doing good in school and honing his writing. He lives well outside of Toronto with his mother and her cat while maintaining a long-distance relationship with his girlfriend Misty (aka Éowyn16). His ultimate goal is to top the e-book charts on web site Amazon.com.

ONE

It was a damp and foamy night. Mr. and Mrs. Dunkley, of number four, Pervert Drive, were proud to say that they were perfectly normal, thank you very much. They were the last people you'd expect to be involved in anything kinky or weird, because they just didn't hold with such nonsense. Which is why Mrs. Dunkley was quite shocked by what she saw when she opened the door to the room in the sub-basement under the stairs to ask Peter to go clean the leaves off the roof.

"Dangit, Auntie Eve! You're supposed to knock!" shouted Peter.

Mrs. Dunkley covered her eyes as Peter covered up his crotch with the teddy bear that he had been sitting on as he masturbated.

"I, uh," Mrs. Dunkley stammered, "it's raining very hard outside, and, uh …"

Peter mashed at his netbook computer's keyboard with one hand, but he couldn't get rid of the animated video of two winged demon women smooshing their oversized breasts together.

Mrs. Dunkley kept a hand over her eyes, angling it so she could only look at the floor. "Uh, the eavestroughs are overflowing again, so, get up there and scoop the leaves out. Please."

"Okay, okay, I'll just be a second," said Peter. One of the demon women moaned as a forked tongue caressed her pointy nipple.

"Dear God, Peter," said Mrs. Dunkley as she slammed the door.

Peter sighed. Usually he could hear his aunt's footsteps coming down the stairs and cover up before she arrived, but the rain slamming against the house must have covered up the sound.

He turned back to his computer. The video was just getting to the good part. He put his teddy bear back down on the bed, sat on it (it wasn't weird, he just liked the texture of it), then finished up as quickly as he could. He blew his load into a dirty sock, then tossed it under the bed.

After getting his clothes on, he headed upstairs. Mr. and Mrs. Dunkley stopped whispering as he passed the living room. From the veins sticking out of Mr. Dunkley's forehead, Peter could tell that Mrs. Dunkley had told him what happened.

"You nearly killed your aunt," he said through clenched teeth.

"She should have knocked," said Peter as he got on his hole-ridden rain coat.

"This is our house. Your aunt can go where she damn well pleases. You just turned the legal age of consent, and we only agreed to keep you here for a few years after your parents exploded."

Peter popped his jacket's hood over his shaggy hair. "I'm trying to find a job," he mumbled.

Mr. Dunkley exhaled through his large nostrils. "Soon you'll be *trying* to find shelter. Because you won't have it here." Mrs. Dunkley stared at the carpet.

Peter opened his mouth to say something, but nothing would come out. He groaned, then stepped out into the rain, slamming the door behind him. The mud squished around his shoes as he made his way around the little white house, his old sneakers soaking right through. He was nearly at the ladder around the back when he thought of what he should have said to his uncle: *well then who's going to do all your chores?* When his uncle had threatened to kick him out. He should have said that.

Feeling totally sad, he climbed the ladder, sure to skip the eighth rung, which fell out whenever he stepped on it. On the roof, he could barely see through the frothy rain whipping against his face. He kneeled and felt his way around the edge. A sheet of water splashed against his knees, then continue to the overflowed eavestrough, then down to the ground, where it threatened to flood the basement again, then drip down into Peter's room in the sub-basement.

In the dark, he couldn't immediately see the blockage, but he found his way to where it usually was, and, sure enough, there was a wad of leaves blocking the little gutter. He began scooping it out and throwing it to the ground. Black rottenness smeared on his hands, and insects crawled up his arms.

Peter lifted another clump of leaves and reared back to toss it to the ground. Behind, something thumped against the roof. He turned and squinted, but he could barely see where the shingles ended and the sky began in the moist darkness.

He shuffled as he turned back around, but as he went to toss the leaves, one of his knees slipped, and he found himself tumbling forward. Before he knew what was happening, he'd done a somersault, then there was only air and rain in front of him. Well fuck, he was going to break his neck. Die a virgin.

Something clamped around Peter's ankle, stopping his fall. He wriggled, trying to look up, but all he could see was a dark shape outlined by the splash of raindrops. Near the top of that dark shape were two glowing blue eyes.

"Gotcha," said a deep voice from above. Peter began to rise.

Dragged back onto the roof, a massive mass towered above him. Those glowing blue eyes weren't his imagination.

"Peter Harrison?" asked the deep voice.

"Yes," Peter squeaked.

"Ah, found ya. Just in time, looks like. I'm Hardrod." A meaty hand emerged from under the giant man's overcoat. Peter shook it, but he could only get a grip on a few of the sausage-ish fingers.

"I've come to give you a lift," said Hardrod. "To the school. You know, like it said in your letter."

"Letter?"

"Yeah I know, I'm early. But the letter explained all this."

"Is a letter, like, a paper email?" asked Peter.

Hardrod grunted. "Let's get out of the rain. We can talk on the way." He turned and stomped up the incline of the roof, then over the peak to the other side. Peter scrambled up after him. As he got to the other side, he saw Hardrod getting into the back of a windowless white van parked on the roof.

"Whaaat?" said Peter.

"Get in," said Hardrod.

Peter could hear his aunt and uncle squawking out front. They'd probably heard the van thump down on the roof, and the sound of Hardrod's footsteps. "If that little asshole fell off and died, I'm going to kill him," Peter heard his uncle bluster.

Peter sighed. "Fuck it," he mumbled, then got into the back of the van.

Hardrod closed the sliding door behind him, then hunkered onto a bench along a wall of the featureless interior of the van. Peter sat on the bench opposite him. With the overhead light on, Peter got a better look at Hardrod. He was a tall, chubby man with a pasty face and a sparse beard that looked like someone glued pubes on a cantaloupe.

The van's ignition turned, then it began to move. Peter turned to see who was driving, but the driver's compartment was blocked off. Then he realized they were still on a roof, and braced himself for the van crashing to the ground.

But no, the van did not crash. He felt himself pushed down instead of up, because yeah, the van was totally flying.

Hardrod shook himself like a wet dog, spraying Peter with yet another layer of moisture. His deep voice rumbled: "Must be exciting, eh? Been reading about self-driving vehicles all your life, but probably never been in one yourself, eh?"

“Self-driving cars? Like from Google?”

Hardrod laughed. “That’s a funny word.”

Peter suddenly felt very trapped in the windowless van. What the hell had he gotten himself into? He shivered.

“Must be cold in those wet clothes,” said Hardrod.

“Nah, I’m okay,” said Peter.

“I insist!” bellowed Hardrod.“I’ve got something more comfortable you can slip into.” He reached across the van and grabbed the bottom of Peter’s jacket. Peter struggled, but the beefy hands were so big, Hardrod might as well have been getting a baby undressed.

Soon, the giant man had taken off Peter’s jacket and shirt. Hardrod’s beady brown eyes flicked up and down; Peter could feel the man scanning the wet, matted patches of body hair.

Hardrod broke into a big smile. “You’re a hairy wizard!”

TWO

Cold wind slashed at Peter's face. "What the crap are you doing?" he asked, yelling to compete with the rushing air.

"We're almost there. Thought you might like the view!" bellowed Hardrod, pushing the other back door of the van open.

It *was* quite the view. The van soared over a blanket of treetops, yellow and orange from autumn, bathed in morning light. The forest spread out as far as Peter could see in every direction—except one direction, in which trees abruptly gave way to greyish water. That was the direction in which they headed, the van getting lower and lower until he felt like he could reach out and touch the branches below. He held tight onto his seat.

"There it is," said Hardrod, pointing a hotdog-resembling finger in the direction of the water.

There it was: an old mansion, perched on a rocky ledge above the ocean. The van passed it, then began to circle back. Above the cave-pocked cliff, the mansion's balconies hung over the water. The sheer sides were adorned with small windows. Towers at its corners seemed to anchor it to the rock. The mansion had been white once, but the paint peeled so much that it looked like it was spotted. Along the front, a quartet of columns made up its facade. As the van slowed and touched down in front of the mansion, Peter saw that the columns were topped with a round, mushroom-like tip instead of the usual Doric capitals.

Peter wore a bath robe, which Hardrod had given him after stripping him out of his wet clothes. He hugged it tight, then stood to get out of the van.

A woman emerged from the double doors behind the mushroom columns. Her curly red hair sprung in the wind as she approached, clutching the purple bath robe that she wore to keep it from flying open.

Hardrod helped Peter out of the van. The woman scanned him up and down with bulbous violet eyes that lingered as they aimed at his crotch. He realized he'd been staring at her, and his own bath robe had flapped open, revealing his wet underwear and the bulge underneath. He grabbed the robe's flap and bunched it over himself.

"Hm, nice," said the woman. Whether she was sarcastic or just confident, Peter couldn't tell. "I'm Maggie," said the woman, who was Maggie.

"This is Peter," said Peter. "Er, I mean, I am Peter."

She raised one eyebrow. "Welcome. I teach Transfigurbation here and I am the dean of student relations. We'll wait until the whole batch of students has arrived before showing you around. You know what to expect, don't you?"

"I really don't, miss."

She laughed; a husky but soothing sound. She seemed to realize that Peter wasn't laughing along with her.

"Where *did* you get this one, Hardrod?"

Hardrod opened his mouth to answer, but was interrupted by a rumbling from the sky. Other vans approached from various directions, each of them as white and windowless as the one Peter had ridden in on. None had drivers. The steering wheels spun themselves, aiming the vans to touch down in the courtyard around the mansion.

Peter had a moment of panic as he realized that everybody here seemed to expect him to know what he was doing. He'd never even considered wizardry to be real, except for the conspiracy theories on the Internet. He'd never seen a flying vehicle drive itself. He'd never cast a spell. He'd never even had sex!

Oops, he was staring at Maggie again.

The doors to the vans opened. Guys spilled out, each of them about Peter's age, each of them wearing bath robes. They all had big smiles on their faces as they stepped out, as if they'd been waiting for this their whole lives.

Peter thought that maybe if he could just go with the flow, pretend he knew what he was doing, then things would be okay. Awesome, even.

He was totally wrong.

***

Maggie led the new students up the steps and through the double doors of the mansion.

"Welcome to Argus Felch's School of Wizarding," she said. The guys around them whispered to each other. Peter caught snippets: "wasn't in the brochures;" "who is Argus Felch?" A guy with shaggy red hair turned to Peter and said, "not quite what I expected."

The foyer had once been majestic, but was looking run-down. Wood showed through the white paint of the stairway curving to a second-floor landing. The marble floors were layered with dirt and footprints. A broom sat by the front door, but it must have been used for transportation rather than cleaning up.

"I'd like silence, please," said Maggie, her voice deep, booming, but alluringly feminine. "Dinner is this way, boys."

At the mention of food, the guys seemed to relax. They followed Maggie to another set of double doors leading off the main foyer. Her butt wiggled under her bath robe and her high heeled shoes clacked against the marble floor, echoing throughout the room.

"Mind your heads as we go in here," she said, wrenching the creaky doors open.

The room blew Peter's mind. Folding tables were set up in what had once been a gymnasium. About twenty guys were already seated at them. Upon a stage at the far end, a wooden table was covered in food. The part that was surprising, though, was the candles that lit the room; they floated in mid-air.

Peter's mouth gaped in awe as he walked in, trying to understand what was holding the candles up. Then a sharp pain hit him in the forehead. Hot wax sizzled as he shouted in pain.

"Told you to mind your head," muttered Maggie, looking back at Peter with a crooked smile.

The other guys timed their entrance to avoid the dripping wax and shuffled around the mounds of it on the floor.

"Here, I'll get it," said the red-haired guy beside Peter. He wiped off the hot wax with the sleeve of his robe. "I'm Rod. Rod Williesby."

"Thanks, Rod Williesby. I'm Peter. Peter Harrison."

"Brilliant," said Rod for some reason. He followed Peter into the room, where the two of them sat together at one of the empty tables. The other guys—especially the current students who were already seated—avoided eye contact with Peter. Were they onto him? Did they know he wasn't actually a wizard?

Older people in embroidered bath robes entered the room and shuffled onto the stage to take places at the head table. Maggie joined them, sitting beside a larger, empty chair near the centre. She raised one of her hands, then the current students immediately fell silent. The new class took a moment longer to shut up.

"Thank you," said Maggie. "Grand Wizard Felch will not be joining us tonight. However, I would like to personally welcome our new class of students to Argus Felch's School of Wizarding. Please, boys, let's get a round of applause to make them all feel at home."

The current students clapped politely.

"Now, let's eat!"

Carts rolled into the gymnasium, pushed by very short people wearing leather body suits. Even their faces were covered by the head-to-toe leather, with holes only for their eyes and noses.

Peter must have been making a face. Rod turned to him. "I've never seen one in person either. A house ALF. They do look different than in the brochures though, don't they? They don't usually wear those silly costumes. I suppose each school is different though, isn't it?"

"I, uh, yes, I suppose that is correct," said Peter, still staring at the ALFs. They stopped at each table to distribute food from the carts, carefully placing the trays down with their tiny gloved hands.

"Oy, right on, chicken hoagies," said Rod. "Wizards love chicken hoagies, don't they?"

"Do they?"

"Right. Me mum always made 'em for me, but I bet they're magically delicious here. Probably got some flavour wizards working in the kitchen."

The food did look delicious. The bun was a perfect oval with sesame seeds distributed in a perfect grid. The chicken in the middle was formed into a deep-fried patty that fit the bun exactly, with vegetables, sauce, and cheese that poked out from the bun just enough to make their presence known, but not enough to get messy. The whole thing glistened slightly in the candlelight. It looked just like the food in the flyers that Peter used to look through when Aunt Eve and Uncle Tony made him go get the mail. Each drop of moisture on the cheese globules looked like it was placed there with an eye dropper.

The fries were equally perfect, each one exactly the same 2x4 shape. He popped one into his mouth.

Rod did the same. He frowned.

Peter swallowed. "I wouldn't call them magically delicious."

“Not quite.” Rod took a bite of the chicken hoagie, chewed, then said with his mouth still full, “Not good. Not good.”

A guy at another table turned toward Peter and Rod. “Shhh!” he said. He was one of the current students. “Don’t complain. You want them hearing you? Just eat and keep your heads down.”

“Right, okay, don’t want to insult them on our first day here,” said Peter.

The guy rolled his eyes, then went back to mechanically chewing his food.

Peter and Rod raised their eyebrows at each other, then stifled laughter.

“Tell you what,” said Rod, quietly. “I’ve got something better that I brought from home. Managed to grab a few and stuff me pockets before they put me in the van. Let's hang out later and I’ll share with you.”

“Sounds like a plan,” said Peter.

He noticed that Maggie was staring at him from the head table.

The teachers’ food looked just as good as the students’, but they seemed to be enjoying it more. Maggie plucked a piece of moist pink steak from a fork with her equally moist pink lips, then swallowed it whole, making eye contact with Peter the whole time.

He looked away and felt himself blush. She must have been suspicious of him.

The next time he hazarded a look up, she again turned her attention to him. She picked up a baby carrot with her orange-painted nails, held it to her lips, and gave it a soft kiss right on the tip.

Peter felt himself getting stiff.

Maggie slid the baby carrot past her most moistest lips. Then she swallowed the whole thing in one gulp.

Peter’s jaw dropped. He realized he still had a mouthful of hoagie in his mouth, and snapped it shut.

Maggie raised one of her perfectly sculpted eyebrows and smiled with one side of her mouth.

She knew. She knew he wasn't a wizard. Why else would she be staring at him, out of all the guys in this room?

"—brownie?" Rod had been talking to him.

"Huh? What?" asked Peter.

"You gonna eat your brownie? It's the best part. Guess it's hard to bugger up sweets."

Peter absent-mindedly reached for the perfect cube of dough and icing sitting on his tray, then began to hand it to Rod with a shaking hand. He couldn't handle it any more.

"I'm not a wizard!" tumbled out of his mouth. At least he managed to keep it down to a whisper.

"Whot?" asked Rod halfway through a bite of brownie.

"I have no idea what I'm doing here," said Peter.

"Right then, that's gonna be a problem, isn't it?"

THREE

Maggie emphasized that there would be no wandering the halls at night. The students would be led to their dorms, where they would find an itinerary for tomorrow, Monday. They could socialize in the common areas of their suites, and they could read the books on the shelves there, but they were absolutely not to wander the halls at night.

Also, they weren't allowed to jerk off.

Maggie explained: "We have magical sperm detectors that will alert us if you choke your chicken, shake your snake, or wiggle your walrus. This is a serious school, and we will not have distractions. It's also been a problem for the cleaning staff. The shower drains clogged up so bad that it flooded the basement. So please refrain from ticking your pickle, slamming your salami, or cuffing your carrot."

Peter found that a bit strange, but he supposed it was a small price to pay for learning goddamn magic. Still, he anticipated having trouble with the rule. Especially when Maggie looked directly at him as she said *carrot.*

The boys were led to their dorms. Rod stayed near Peter, so that when one of the ALFs pointed at the nearest two students, then assigned them to the nearest room, the two of them became roommates.

"Roomies! Brilliant!" said Rod.

Their dorm was a small common area surrounded by two private rooms and one bathroom. The common area held a couch, a table, a bookshelf, a bar fridge, and not much else. Rod collapsed on the couch and let out a sigh. Peter joined him.

After a moment of silence, Rod jumped up again. "Oooh yeah! I promised you I had some better food, didn't I?"

"You did."

He reached into a pocket of his bath robe and pulled out two wrapped packages. "Chocolate boobs," he said.

"Rad. I like chocolate and I like boobs," said Peter.

"Ah but you said you're not a wizard, didn't you?"

"I did."

"So you've probably never seen chocolate boobs like these." He unwrapped a pair of them and placed them on the table. The unnaturally round breasts moved on their own, bouncing up and down in what Peter imagined to be a realistic manner.

"Wow," said Peter. "That's pretty cool. But, um, what's the point?"

"Magic, Peter! It doesn't always make sense. Don't you like to play with your food before you eat it?" Rod picked up the boobs and flicked at a quivering nipple with his tongue before taking a big bite out of it.

Peter laughed, for the first time that day. "Okay, okay, give me one," he said. The chocolate was probably the best Peter had ever tasted, though the sensation of having it jiggle as he put it in his mouth was an odd one. He imagined it was similar to French kissing.

"So, you excited for tomorrow?" asked Rod through a mouthful of chocolate.

"I guess. Dude, to be honest, I'm terrified. I don't know how I ended up here. I'm not a wizard. I'd never even heard of real wizards before."

"Right," said Rod. "I've been looking forward to this my whole life. My father wizarded back in England; met my mother while wizarding for charity. They always told me that shortly after I turned the legal age of consent in my country or jurisdiction, they'd come to whisk me away to wizarding school. From what I hear it's all pretty automatic. Maybe they mistook you for someone else? They wouldn't just pick up a random Subble or Guzzle."

"Subble? Guzzle?"

"Non-magic folks. Guzzles steal power from real wizards. Always at war with us, they are. Right, it doesn't matter. Let's just figure out how to get you faking it until we figure out how you ended up here."

Peter's uneasy stomach rumbled. He tasted chocolate in his burp. "Fake it? Shouldn't I just tell them?"

"Crikey, no. Wizards don't treat non-magic folks very well. And in case you didn't notice, I don't think we got placed in the friendliest of schools here."

Peter felt sick. "I should just run."

Rod must have seen how pale Peter was. "Calm down, roomie. They don't let the new students do magic until later anyway, so you'll be okay for the first few classes. I'll be here to help you out if you're falling behind. It'll be just fine, won't it?"

"I dunno."

"Won't it?"

“Okay, okay, it will be just fine.”

Rod smiled. “I’m here for you.”

But Peter felt his heart racing in his chest. He told Rod that he was tired, thanked him for being such a good roomie, then headed towards his room.

He really wanted to jerk off. It would calm him down enough to sleep. Then he pictured Maggie saying "please refrain from tickling your pickle." Then he wanted to jerk off even more.

He opened the door to his room feeling homesick already, just wanting something to comfort him. When he saw his bed, he gasped at what was there.

It was his teddy bear from back home. Somehow, it had showed up on his bed in wizarding school.

FOUR

The first week of classes was shockingly familiar.

Peter thought he'd be blown away by this world of magic that he'd been whisked away into. But the wizarding life was not all that different from the life he was used to. One of the classes was, as far as he could tell, just algebra. Another was not unlike English, except the books they analyzed were purposefully devoid of anything magical or fantastical.

At least in the equivalent of biology class, they learned more about the ALFs. Without their masks, apparently, they were ugly little bear-like creatures with patchy hair and pig-like snouts, rumoured to be from another planet. Peter perked up when the teacher said this, but the other students all seemed bored.

Peter thought the teachers would be quirky eccentrics with elaborate tales of magical adventures. But they were even more apathetic than his college professors were before he dropped out. Most of them opted to have the students read textbooks in silence instead of actually teaching anything at all. The most eccentric thing was that half of them drank on the job, sipping from tiny flasks when they thought students weren't looking.

At least he could fit in. Since there was no actual magic going on, Peter was just another slightly-less-bored student among a bunch of guys raised as wizards.

The teachers kept him interested. All of them were women, and almost all were gorgeous. Peter often found himself staring at Ms. Spout's tattoos, peeking out of her robes on her toned arms, or Mrs. Trelaney's soft lips and shiny blonde hair, or even grey-haired old Madam Olorin's weirdly sag-free boobs.

Rod said he couldn't see what Peter saw in the teachers; they reminded him too much of his mom. But for Peter, their beauty made the nights even harder to deal with. After Friday's last class, he rushed to the bathroom to take a massive dump, where a sign inside the stall reminded him once again: No masturbating. A crude drawing of a penis with a hand around it was covered by a big red X. Below that, *magical sperm detectors installed. Violators will be penalized.*

Despite the sign, he found his hand reaching down as he pictured Ms. Spout's hints of tattoos, enticing him further into the folds of her robe. He wondered how far those tattoos went. If they swirled around her breasts.

He wrenched his pants up. No. He was trying to avoid attention, and breaking the rules in the first week wouldn't help.

There was a social gathering that night in the gymnasium, once again filled with tables and lit by candles.

Rod showed up a few minutes late, chatting with another student wearing a red bath robe.

"Peter, have you met Mathieu? He sits behind us in Cryptobuggery."

The way Rod said it, Mathieu's name rhymed with *achoo.*

"Nice to meet you," said Mathieu.

"'Sup," said Peter.

The three of them sat at the end of the table sipping the Diet Coke that was provided as the sole entertainment for the gathering. The new students had already formed into cliques, bunching up in chatty groups of three or four. The older students, however, sat in near silence, only occasionally leaning to one side to whisper to the people beside them.

"It's not really what we were promised, is it?" asked Peter.

Mathieu shook his head. "Nope. My mom told me stories about her wizarding education. She went on field trips to Monster Island. Her class mastered the Avadickavera spell in their first week. And one of her teachers was Schmegdick the Magician! Can you believe that?"

"Whoa, really?" said Rod, his mouth dropping open.

Peter laughed awkwardly. "Wow, Schmegdick. Crazy," he said.

Rod leaned in close to Peter and winked at Mathieu. "It's okay Peter, you don't have to pretend. I already told Mathieu about your, uh, history, or lack of it."

"Oh," said Peter. "Okay." He frowned. Why the hell did Rod spill his secret without even talking to him first? In fact, even though he promised to help Peter out, Rod had been mostly absent during classes, sometimes sitting with other guys, only chatting with Peter once they got back to their dorm.

"I was shocked, quite frankly," said Mathieu. "I don't know how you ended up here. You'll be in massive trouble if they find out."

“Thanks, Mathieu. Real comforting."

Rod laughed. "Peter'll be fine. Looks like this dump will be miserable for all of us anyway. Might as well enjoy it, right? Cheers, mates." He lifted his plastic cup full of Diet Coke.

Mathieu tapped his glass against Rod's. Peter reluctantly lifted his, too.

They hadn't been there for an hour when Maggie appeared on the stage.

“Sorry, boys, social time is over," she said. "Return to your rooms. Your weekend will be best spent studying. I have been assured by all the teachers that there will be pop quizzes shortly."

Peter followed Rod and Mathieu as they walked toward the door, chatting excitedly about how their families celebrated various wizarding holidays.

Mathieu turned to Peter. “Oh, you probably don’t even know what Durpin’s Day is. It’s okay though, you’ll be able to join in the celebrations even if you aren’t, you know, a real wizard.”

“Peter!” Maggie was directly behind them.

Peter whirled around, hoping that she hadn't heard Mathieu out him, but she was close enough that she might have.

"Yes, ma'm?"

She swished her hand at Rod and Mathieu. They kept walking. She put a hand on Peter's shoulder. "How was your first week? Fitting in?"

"Yep!" said Peter, maybe too quickly. "Fitting in just fine, with all these wizards. Great being a wizard, um, isn't it?"

She arched one of her sculpted eyebrows. "Yes, Peter, it is. You come to me if you need anything, okay?"

Peter nodded.

Maggie studied his face, as if she were searching it for something. Did wizards have some kind of mark that he was missing? Extra nipples where their animal companions suckled? She reached out, lightly touched his cheek. "If you need me, come."

Her hand felt like velvet on his face. "Thanks!" he said, then turned to leave before she could see the front of his robe beginning to poke up. He hurried to his room, half-expecting her to follow him, grab him, and toss him out into the cold—or worse—but when he looked back, she was gone.

Rod wasn't in the common room when Peter got back. "You alright?" mumbled Rod through the open door to his own room.

"I … I think so."

"Brilliant," mumbled Rod. "Night night, then."

Peter wanted somebody to talk to. Somebody to, like, bounce ideas off of. Maybe plan an escape before the wizards discovered his secret, if they hadn't already. But he was very tired, and Rod didn't appear to want to chat.

He sighed, then headed to his room. Cuddling his teddy bear, feeling very alone, he silently sobbed until he felt his eyes closing, his mind drifting, peace starting to creep in.

Then the snoring started.

FIVE

It sounded like a bear with diarrhea.

He'd feel sleep coming on—his mind bringing him visions of Maggie's soft hand on his face, then fingertipping lower and lower—when Rod's nose and throat would explode, ripping Peter back into terrifying reality.

It sounded like a pig being slaughtered in a tub of Play-Dough.

In a moment of silence, his half-dreams provided him with an image of Maggie slowly slipping her robe off of her shoulders, lower, lower, a pink hint of nipple appearing, and then: a torrent of sloshing phlegm and drool awoke him like a bucket of water to the face.

Peter needed to leave. He'd always thought blue balls were a myth, but they ached like they'd been stomped on by the bear with diarrhea.

He opened the dorm door slowly, making sure it didn't creak. Nobody was in the dark hallway. Wandering the halls at night was not allowed, but surely they didn't have anybody staying up all night to enforce that. And surely the magical sperm detectors that kept him from jerking off in his own room would not be in *every* bathroom.

The nearest bathroom was a few halls over, past the dorms of the older students and other halls that branched off to who-knows-where. Peter walked on the edges of his feet, avoiding even the swish of socks against linoleum.

He could see a washroom sign at the end of the hall. Only one, since the students were all males, and the staff must have had washrooms in their rooms. He pussy-footed forward, and was almost halfway there when he saw a flickering light getting brighter at the end of the hallway. Someone was coming from another corridor.

Peter turned and stepped back where he came from as quickly but quietly as he could. He wasn't quick enough.

"Peter." A woman. He turned around. Maggie.

She held a lantern with a ball of light floating in the middle. The light flickered on and off with a quiet buzz, like an old fluorescent light. Peter stood with his arms crossed in front of him, feeling his face redden, until she arrived.

He sputtered: "I was just uh—roommate clogged the toilet, needed to find another. He's, um, a bear—I mean—he had um, diarrhea." His face was so red, it was a good thing the lantern was dim.

"So you were heading to that bathroom then, were you?" Her eyebrow arched, as if she were gesturing behind her with it.

“Yes, ma'm. To pee, I mean."

"To pee."

"Yes."

She sighed, but a smile formed on her face. "Come, let's go to the bathroom then. I'd like to show you something.”

Peter brushed his shaggy hair from his sweaty forehead and followed her to the bathroom. The silhouette of her butt swishing in front of him was enough to send blood rushing to his aching genital region.

They entered the small stone-walled bathroom with two dim light bulbs hanging above the mirror. Maggie latched the door behind them.

“Peter, do you remember when I said there was to be no wandering the halls at night?”

“Yes, but—“

She interrupted him. “Peter, do you see this sign on the wall?”

Violators will be penalized. “Yes. Yes! But I was only coming to pee!”

Her hand was suddenly on his crotch. “Peter, your staff is already stiff. I don’t believe that you were only coming to urinate.”

His face reddened again, but her hand felt warm on the front of his robe. He opened his mouth to explain, but nothing came out.

"Let me inspect your staff," said Maggie. She pushed him against the wall in front of the sink, then undid the knot holding his robe closed. She looked him up and down, everything exposed except what was covered by his boxers. His nappy chest hair and fuzzy belly.

"You're a hairy wizard," she said.

"I can expl—"

She put a finger to his mouth. "Hush. Let's get a closer inspection."

With her long, delicate fingers, she pinched the edge of his boxers, then slipped them down. His "staff" snapped out of his boxers so fast that he expected an audible *boing!*

Maggie gripped his penis between two slender fingers and moved it to the left, then right, her eyes fixated on it.

"Impressive," she said.

Peter's heart slammed in his chest so hard he could feel his staff trying to bob up and down in her hand. "Miss, m'am, if I've done something wrong—"

"Oh Peter, cut the shit. I've seen the way you look at me. Will you just relax?"

His face was more flushed than ever, but he managed to exhale. "Okay."

"Okay. You want this, don't you?" she asked. Her tongue, redder than her hair, flicked out from between her lips, coming within millimetres of his cock.

Peter nodded. "Yes."

"I want this too." She exhaled, the warmth of her breath tickling his cock and causing it to surge in her hand like a bucking bronco (except smaller). "Yes. Yes, I want your sperms, Peter."

Her lips opened again, then enveloped Peter. Suddenly all his worry about being a fraud, all his embarrassment at being caught in the hallway, all his anger at Rod, it all melted away as he slid in and out.

She moved slowly, her tongue wriggling up and down his cock like a sexual snake on a log. He got close to coming right then, but she seemed to sense it and slowed her pace further.

"Uuuunh," said Peter, which was the sound of moaning.

She pulled back and gave his cock a quick lick on the way out, almost sending him over the edge again, but he held back.

"You like this?"

"Yes."

"Then give me something in return. Give me your come."

He nodded as she wrapped her face around him again, increasing her pace. He instinctively moved his hips back and forth, pistoning in rhythm with her movements, entering and exiting like Jesus popping in and out of his tomb every year at Easter.

"Oh God," he moaned.

She started going faster and deeper. It was only the novelty of the experience that kept him from splooging immediately. He could see his own cock making her throat bulge unnaturally. He couldn't believe he was being deep-throated, like in the movies he watched on mute in his uncle's sub-basement.

She let it in even deeper, her lips hitting the very base of his staff. Then deeper still, his testicles slipping into her mouth. It hurt a bit, but also felt good a bit. She let his cock and balls pop in and out of her mouth a few times, then pulled back.

A string of drool bridged from her mouth to his cock, then collapsed and splatted on her chest, dripping into the cleavage now visible due to the looser flaps of her purple robe.

She poked the tip of his penis up, examining it closely with her large violet eyes. One of her eyebrows went up in that extremely sexy way it always did.

"You're close, aren't you? Give it to me now."

Peter thrust forward. She opened her mouth just in time for him.

One of her red curls got caught in the action. It was dragged into her mouth by his cock. For some reason, that was what sent Peter over the edge.

He leaned back as warmth overtook his body. The cold stone wall behind him made his butt hole clench, increasing the power of his oncoming orgasm.

The bathroom lights became brighter for a moment. Peter felt a herd of sperms surging forth from his testicles. He tried to pull back and spray onto Maggie's face, like in the pornography movies, but she scrambled forward with a hungry look in her eyes and clamped onto the tip of his cock.

His ball sack constricted. Come began to pump. The light bulbs above the bathroom mirror exploded in a shower of yellow sparks, but Peter barely noticed because it felt really, really good.

The first pump was almost too much for Maggie to handle. Globs of it squirted out around the edges of his shaft, joining the wetness already on her chest. But then his sack constricted again, sending another pump into Maggie's mouth. This time she opened her throat in time.

Come continued to pump, and Maggie swallowed. Her eyes rolled back in ecstasy. Gulp, gulp, gulp, her throat bulged as she drank.

Peter's nuts became smaller with each contraction, until they were nearly empty.

Maggie released his cock, then tilted her head back and took one final swallow.

"Thank you, Peter. Your sperms were delectable." She stood, turned to the sink, and grabbed a wad of paper towel from the dispenser to wipe the drool and come off her chest.

Peter didn't know what to say. "I don't know what to say," he said.

"Don't say anything, dear. Just be a good student and go back to your room. Wandering the halls at night is forbidden." She tightened her purple robe, then turned to leave.

Peter stood against the wall, pushing into it as if it were the only thing keeping him up. He felt wobbly all over.

Maggie picked up her lantern; the ball of light in it was twice as bright and had lost its flicker. As she opened the door to leave, Maggie turned back. "Oh, Peter?"

"Hmm?" he said, his voice squeaking.

Her gaze flicked down, then back up. "You might want to cover up before you go?"

His flaccid dick was still hanging from his open robe like a deflated party balloon. "Yes!" he said. "Okay. Um, should we … talk about this?"

She laughed, a husky yet cold sound, as she closed the door behind her.

***

Peter's legs were still wobbly as he left the bathroom. His mind wandered. He turned a corner, then another, and soon realized that he was completely lost.

He came across a flickering EXIT sign leading to a stairwell he hadn't seen before. An idea popped into his head: he'd go downstairs to the front door, then take the familiar path back up to his room. The stairwell was a circular tower spiralling up and down. When Peter reached the first floor landing, he noticed that the stairs kept going down. Curiosity got the better of him.

There weren't any classes below the main floor, and he'd never seen anybody go into the basement. The walls became rough as he descended. Ancient mossy stones replaced tidy bricks. He came to the floor below the main level, guarded by a heavy door made of steel and wood. The stairs kept going, descending further into the Earth.

A thud echoed from down there. Peter jumped, then scampered back up the stairs. Getting caught wandering by somebody else probably wouldn't go as nicely as it did with Maggie.

The stairwell filled with a jingling sound, and among that, heavy footsteps. Peter paused at the main floor and peeked around the curve of the stairwell. A light approached.

A man rounded the bend. He was the first man Peter had seen here, aside from the students, and occasionally seeing Hardrod puttering about. And there was only one other man that he'd heard about living here: Argus Felch. The founder of the school.

Felch had a deeply lined face and scraggly grey hair that was currently hanging off his head in wet strings. Necklaces of various shapes and sizes hung around his neck, all sparkling in the light from his lantern. The jewelry jingled as he shuffled up the stairs, covering the sound of Peter's steps as he backed away, watching from the darkness.

"Damn thing," muttered Felch. "Won't accept my offerings. Ain't trying to hurt it. It'll realize, yes yes, it'll realize soon."

Felch paused at the door to the first basement level. Dark spots formed on the stone below him; he was soaking wet, his bath robe heavy with water that dripped as he stood there. He grabbed a wand from a loop in his robe and muttered some unintelligible words as he pointed it at the heavy door. It swung open on its own. Continuing to mutter miserably, he walked through the door, which shut itself behind him.

Peter thought he heard a shout, but it was faint, from even further down the stairs. He couldn't tell if it was a bout of laughter, a cry of pain, or just the wind whistling through crevices.

Feeling utterly confused and light-headed, he scrambled back up the stairs, then found his way back to his room. Rod was still snoring like a bear. With all that noise, and the fact that his head was swimming with newly formed questions and memories of new experiences, Peter thought he'd never fall asleep, but as soon as he flopped into bed and grabbed his teddy bear, he was out cold.

SIX

The Quiddix "pitch" was an overgrown field overlooking the ocean. The sun shone, and even though the wind still had bite to it, the boys were happy when Mrs. Trelaney went knocking on doors to get them outside. *Growing boys need physical activity to stay healthy and reach the full potential of their magical output*, she'd said, her fine blond hair waving in the wind as she led them outside.

Hardrod stood on a grassy mound. The sparse curly hairs on his jowls quivered as he talked:

"I'm sure you all seen Quiddix before. Well, I'm your coach for this year. All of you grab your brooms and I'll go over the house rules."

There was a rumble of hesitant excitement as each guy grabbed a broom from a pile in the grass. Most of them were missing half of their bristles, and a few of them were actually rakes.

"First rule: avoid the splodgers! Second rule," began Hardrod.

Peter turned to Rod. "I don't know how to play this," he whispered. It was the first time they'd talked all morning. Peter still had bags under his eyes, but Rod had obviously slept well.

"Mate, you'll pick it up in no time. Easy peasy, Quiddix is."

"What's the broom for?" asked Peter. He saw that the other guys were sticking their brooms between their legs.

"Gotta keep your twig 'n berries planted on the broom the whole game. It's your main weapon, and also for magic," said Rod.

"Magic?"

Rod sighed. "It's your wand."

"It's a broom."

Rod grabbed the end of the broom as Peter straddled it. "A wand is anything that's long and hard, to focus the magic, yeah? A broom's as good a wand as a bloody stick."

"… absolutely no snitch-nipping or quaffle-poking …" continued Hardrod.

"Quaffle-poking?!" Peter whispered to Rod.

Rod grumbled. "Just try it out then ask questions later, can't you? You're getting on me gobby nerves."

"Next rule: don't interrupt a beater when he's beating. Hey, who's gonna volunteer to be a beater?"

Rod suddenly whipped his head from side to side. "Mathieu said he'd like to be a beater, but I haven't seen him all day."

Another guy spoke up: "Me neither. He wasn't even at breakfast. Mathieu loves breakfast."

Hardrod scratched his curly beard hairs. "Nothing to worry about, I'm sure. Any other volunteers?"

Peter whispered to Rod. "What's a beater?"

"Oh, for the love of knickerbockers," muttered Rod, then he cleared his throat. Shouting to the whole group, he said, "Peter wants to be a beater!"

That asshole! Peter shook his head, but already he was being pushed to the front. The other guys insisted that Rod be the other beater, and he reluctantly accepted. Peter found himself in front of the whole class, with Rod, that jerk who used to be his friend but who had almost outed him as a non-wizard several times now, beside him.

"Just follow my lead; it'll be fine," whispered Rod.

Hardrod pointed out the two goals: holes dug into the lumpy ground, surrounded by red plastic rings. Balls of various colours were placed throughout the field. He split the group into two, then told half to take their robes off, because they were the skins team.

Peter was on the skins team. As he slipped down to his underwear, another guy looked at him and exclaimed, "you're a hairy wizard!"

A whistle blew and the game began.

Quiddix was very confusing. Balls started flying at Peter's face immediately, but he dodged them and kept an eye on Rod. The other guys scooted awkwardly around the field with their brooms between their legs, tossing balls and running into each other. Occasionally, Hardrod would blow a whistle for no discernible reason, then send one guy off the field or bring a new guy on from the sidelines.

A topless guy from Peter's team grabbed one of the blue balls and started running with it to the other side of the field. Rod took off after him. The guy with the blue ball almost reached the goal, but Peter intercepted him and grabbed the end of his broom. Keeping a grip on the shaft, Peter, shook it up and down until the guy came off. He fell, dropped his ball, and then a whistle blew.

Peter took note. It looked like the job of the beater was to grab the shafts of the guys with blue balls.

When the game started again, a guy on the shirts team grabbed the blue ball from where it had been dropped. Peter took off after him, one hand keeping his broom between his legs, the other outstretched to grip the other guy's broom.

Just as Peter was about to grab the shaft, the guy jumped into the air, veering off to the side and sailing past Peter, a smug look on his face. Blue ball in hand, he reached the skins-side goal, leapt in the air again, and landed with the shaft of his broom inside the red hole.

Peter swore. "Fuck" was the word he used.

A whistle blew again. All the guys left the field; it must have been half time.

"Nice try there, mate," said Rod, patting Peter's sweaty, hairy back.

"Thanks," mumbled Peter. He still had no idea what was going on, but he supposed the beater role was the easiest one to figure out, so maybe Rod volunteering him for it wasn't so bad after all.

"Did you see that?" shouted the guy that had scored the goal. His name was Johnny Lawrence or something. "I did magic!"

Peter twisted his face. He hadn't seen anything unusual. "When?" he asked.

"When I jumped past you!" said Johnny. "I changed direction mid-air. Classic inertial extirpation."

"I guess it was a bit of an odd jump," said Peter.

"It was a magical jump!" shouted Johnny, getting up close, the shaft of his broom brushing Peter's thigh.

"Whoa, whoa boys," said Hardrod, stepping between them. "We're all magic here."

Peter sat in the long grass beside Rod, but he didn't seem interested in talking. Rod was being such a dick lately.

"I wonder what the bloody hell happened to Mathieu," mumbled Rod.

"He was gone when I woke up," whispered another guy, presumably Mathieu's roommate.

"Where would he go? There's nothing around," said Rod, gesturing to the grassy fields and forests on one side and the vast ocean on the other.

Peter made sure Hardrod wasn't listening. "Don't you think there's something odd going on with the staff and teachers around here?"

"What do you mean?" asked Rod.

"They seem like they're hiding something. And they're weird around us. The way they ... interact with us."

Peter flashed back to his cock pumping its load into Maggie's mouth, and couldn't help but smile.

"I fancy that you're right," said Rod. "This whole place is very different from what I expected."

"My Rolex watch was missing when I woke up this morning," said another guy who was listening in. "And my door was unlocked. I think there's a thief about."

"And have you noticed that there are way less upper year students than there are us? What happens to them all?" whispered Peter.

Hardrod's whistle interrupted their conversation.

The game continued, but it was clear that the guys didn't have their hearts in it. They had all wanted to be wizards for their entire lives, and probably dreamed of playing Quiddix one day. Running around on brooms in an overgrown field wasn't what they had in mind.

Peter came to a realization. He was different from all the other guys. They had hope. Despite all the disappointment, they knew they would become wizards if they attended classes. They were afraid to upset any of the teachers, because it could put their wizardhood at risk. Peter, however, knew he was not a wizard and never would be. The teachers would figure that out eventually.

In a way, Peter had nothing to lose. If anybody was going to investigate and figure out what was going on here, it would have to be him.

SEVEN

“I’m going to find out what's going on,” Peter said between Rod's snores.

Rod half-opened one eye. "Wha?"

"We all know something is *fishy* around here. Mathieu has gone missing, and I think I heard shouting in the basement last night. I'm going down there on a mission to figure out the mystery behind this story."

"Mission?" asked Rod, his eye drooping closed again.

"Yes," said Peter, frustrated. "I thought I'd tell you where I’m going. In case anything goes wrong. And because you're my friend."

"Sounds good, old chum," said Rod. He rolled over. A moment later he was snoring again.

Peter sighed, said goodbye to his teddy bear, then headed out into the forbidden hallways for the second night in a row. The halls were dark and empty, as usual. He passed the bathroom where he’d had oral sexual relations with Maggie, and smiled. Then frowned.

Why had Maggie come onto him, then let him come into her? Was she testing him? Did she do the same thing with other guys?

Footsteps clomped behind him and he could suddenly see his shadow. For a moment he considered going back to see if it was Maggie again. But no, it sounded like more than one person. He quickened his pace and reached a stairway to the ground floor. The footsteps followed him down.

The door to the makeshift dining room was open, so Peter ducked inside and waited for the people behind him to pass. Peeking out, he saw two figures emerge from the stairwell. One of the house ALFs carried a lantern, and the other carried an empty water jug. It was one of those big transparent jugs, like, the ones that go on a water cooler, you know? The little ALF teetered as he carried it; the bottle was almost as big as he was.

The ALFs passed the doorway. Peter scooted inside. He heard the squeaking of their tight leather body suits as they waddled past.

Peter followed. Maybe the ALFs and the water jugs were clues as to what was going on, and Peter needed clues in order to solve the mystery and complete his mission of finding out what was going on.

The creatures reached the door to the basement. Peter crouched behind a giant wooden goblet softly glowing with blue-white flames. They stopped to look around before going down the stairs. Those things sure were acting suspicious.

He waited a minute, then headed down the basement stairs after them. For the first time since arriving at Felch's School of Wizarding, he felt alive. Like he was doing something important. He swaggered down the stone steps like nobody's business. He was cool, calm, and collected.

In all his swaggering, he didn't see the pool of water in front of the door to the first floor of the basement. His foot shot out from under him and, in an attempt to steady himself, he toppled sideways. Peter found himself tumbling down the stairs, deeper into the basement, toward the glow of the ALFs' lantern and into deeper mysteries.

***

Two blurry faces hovered above Peter's. But they weren't actually blurry, they just looked blurry because Peter had hit his head on the stone floor when he reached the bottom of the staircase, and that made his vision malfunction for a moment.

Anyways, the faces belonged to the ALFs. Peter had been told that the little hairy aliens were suspected to have come from another planet, but he'd never seen what they looked like, due to the leather suits that always covered their faces. Except for now. Their suits had been unzipped and, as they looked down at Peter, he finally got a good look.

They weren't aliens. They were people. Little people. Dwarves. Like that Imp guy from Game of Thrones. And they weren't hairy at all; Peter had more stubble on his face than they did.

"It's that new wizard," said the ALF with the lantern.

"He saw us," said the other ALF as he put down the water jug.

"Grab him."

Each of them grabbed one of his arms. They were strong for their size. Peter tried to struggle, but his head was still foggy and his back hurt from falling down the stairs.

"I thought you dudes were hairy aliens," Peter mumbled as he was dragged through a doorway.

"You're a hairy wizard," said one of the ALFs for some reason.

The stone was cold on Peter's back, and the room smelled musty. The ALFs dragged Peter into an open cavern with barred doors lining the walls. In the middle, a wide stone platform was covered in animal skins. Candles floated under the rocky ceiling; unlike the ones in the dining room, these glowed brightly and were not dripping onto the ground below.

A woman sat cross-legged on the stone platform. A cloud of skunky smoke billowed around her from a long cigarette. As he was thrown at her feet, Peter saw that it was Ms. Spout, his Herbicism teacher.

"Oh, Peter," said Ms. Spout, reaching down to caress the side of his face. "You're not supposed to be here yet."

"Wait, yet?" He sat up. Around the room, pale faces peeked out from between bars. One of them looked like Mathieu's. "What is going on here?" Peter asked, standing up.

The ALFs grabbed him before he could get anywhere. He caught a glimpse of some more of those water jugs sitting on the other side of the stone platform.

"Put him on the bed," commanded Ms. Spout as she stood to make room for him. The ALFs obeyed. Despite the furry animal skin, the "bed" was hard as rock. Because it was made of rock.

Ms. Spout waved her cigarette in the air and mumbled something like "dym re'taz." A plume of smoke burst from the cigarette and flew at Peter. The smoke seemed to gain a mind of its own, splitting in the middle to curl around Peter's hands, becoming solid when it touched his skin. The smoke had transformed into a fine chain. He was fastened to the bed.

"You may go," Ms. Spout said to the ALFs. As they left, another woman came through the doorway. Mrs. Trelaney locked the door shut behind her.

"Are you not done yet, Spout?" asked Trelaney.

"I was, but I had a new visitor stop by." Spout sat on the bed beside Peter.

"Who have we here?" Trelaney approached, rounded the bed, then sat on the other side of Peter. Her long blonde hair smelled like vanilla. She put a bag down beside the water bottle. It fell open and Peter spotted a large piece of rubber in the shape of a penis.

"What the hell is going—"

Ms. Spout put a finger to his lips. "Shush, babe. You must have suspected this isn't a normal wizarding school."

He nodded, his lips smooshing against Spout's finger.

Trelaney caressed his face. "You don't need to worry. You're actually lucky that you stumbled down here. You get to take your turn early."

"My turn?" asked Peter. He glanced around at the barred cells surrounding the cavern.

"Don't worry, all these boys are here willingly," said Spout. "And you are free to go too. Walk out of here now, and the story ends. Go home and believe whatever you want to believe. Stay with us, though, and—"

Trelaney took Peter's chin between her thin fingers and turned his face to her. Her red lips were inches from his. "Stay with us, and we get to show you how deep this rabbit hole goes." She put a knee on the bed and moved closer. "We're offering you the truth of what is going on here. And I promise you'll like it."

"I don't know," said Peter. "I'm not sure I belong here."

Spout looked at Trelaney. "What do you say, Cassie? Should we give him a free sample to see if he likes it?"

"Mmm. We haven't done a double extraction in a while, have we? I think it could increase output from the other boys, too, isn't that right, boys?"

Faces between the cell bars nodded.

Peter recalled his tryst with Maggie. That had turned out okay. If he was going to get booted out of this bizarre school for not being a wizard, he may as well enjoy himself first. He was experiencing so many new things, and isn't that really what school was for?

Spout pulled the belt on her bath robe until the knot came undone. She let the robe flap open. Her bare breasts peeked from the shadows. A tattoo above her left breast seemed to invite Peter to get a closer look.

She leaned back. "Go on, Peter. You're invited to get a closer look."

He pushed the robe out of the way and squeezed her left breast. The chains around his wrists were just long enough to let him move freely. Leaning closer, he saw that the tattoo depicted letters in a strange script. He recognized it as the inscription on The One Ring in Lord of the Rings—the one only revealed by heat. *One ring to rule them all …*

That was so damn cool.

He leaned over and kissed Spout. She lapped at his lips with her tongue for a moment, then pushed him back. "We've got a feisty one, Cassie."

"Mmm. Let's see if he can remain feisty, or if he'll get all soft on us like the other first-timers."

Peter felt his dink become rock-hard, and he was determined to keep it that way. He wasn't a wizard, but maybe he could show these teachers his other skills, gained from years of watching extreme pornography on the Internet.

Trelaney reached into his robe and grabbed his dink. "Still feisty," she said.

He ventured forth with his other hand, squeezing both of Spout's small but soft breasts. Trelaney began to stroke him. He felt himself close to coming already.

"Whoa there," said Trelaney, pulling away. "We want you to come, but we're not quite ready yet."

Spout reached over and undid Trelaney's robe. She slipped out of it, shining blonde hair spilling over her bare shoulders. Her panties had little flowers on them.

Peter switched focus and began to squeeze Trelaney's breasts instead of Spout's. She moaned at his touch.

Spout reached around Peter's shoulders and took off his robe, placing it on the floor beside the stone bed. The bed didn't feel so hard any more. She massaged his fuzzy shoulders as he pleasured Trelaney's nipples and areolae. The skin of the nipple is rich in a supply of special nerves that are sensitive to certain stimuli [Source: Wikipedia, 2014], and he got very excited knowing that she was excited.

"Relax, Peter," said Spout. "This is going to be good for you. You may not learn wizardry here, but you will get to perform magic. When we're done with you, you'll be coming so hard that you'll swear you're the most powerful sorcerer on this God damn planet."

"Mmm hmm," Trelaney moaned. She reached one hand under her flowery panties and pleasured herself, moving in and out of herself with herself. "And all we want from you is your come."

"We want you to come hard, Peter." Spout took Peter's hands off of Trelaney and turned him around. She slipped his underwear off, allowing his bush to spring free. "Can you come hard for us, Peter?"

Peter grinned. "Uh, yep."

Spout slipped out of her panties. Her vagina pounced free. She began to rub it, and Peter found himself rubbing himself as well. Spout's vagina emitted a creamy substance.

"You're going to make me come too," she said.

"Me first!" said Trelaney. She hoisted herself over Peter's face, straddling his head, then pulled her panties to the side and lowered her dripping pussy onto his face. She smelled like flowers and date squares. Tentatively, Peter stuck out his tongue, poking at her lips and mons pubis.

"You haven't done this before, have you?" asked Trelaney.

Determined not to let his virgin secret out, he let instinct take over. His long tongue wriggled up and down until it zeroed in on her clitoris. He once read that tracing out letters with your tongue is the best way to get a lady off, so he traced out the sexiest word he could think of:

W I Z A R D

Trelaney cried out with pleasure. She arched her back, sending sheets of lady-cum pouring over Peter's face.

At the foot of the bed, Spout moaned as well, but she sounded frustrated.

"I need it inside of me," said Spout.

The boys watching from the cells around the room gasped.

“Are you sure that’s a good idea?” asked Trelaney as she eased herself off of Peter’s face with a sexually arousing sucking sound.

“I think our new boy can control himself. Isn’t that right, Peter? You only come when we tell you to come, do you understand?”

“Errr, yup,” said Peter.

Spout straddled Peter. She lowered herself onto him. As soon as he entered her damp lady-cave, he nearly came, but he held it in with all his might. Trelaney looked worried. Spout began to ride him, bouncing up and down on his soft bush of pubic hair. He relaxed, letting himself enjoy it, riding the edge of orgasming.

Spout’s tattooed breast waved up and down, as if in slow motion.

... and in the darkness bind them.

Trelaney leaned over to kiss Peter. She took one of his hands, the magical chain jingling around his wrist, and guided his fingers to her still-sopping pussy. She roughly used his hand for her own pleasure, plunging him in and out as her tongue explored his mouth and Spout’s pussy enveloped his cock.

He wasn’t going to last much longer. He moaned, holding on, careful not to come because they’d told him not to, and if he did he’d probably be exposed as a virgin, or a non-wizard, or both.

His fist clenched. Trelaney took that as an opportunity. She shoved his hand further inside of her, adjusting her position on the bed until he was wrist-deep. Feeling her velvety warmth all around him made his cock clench. His arm stiffened, pushing into Trelaney. His hips jacked, pushing into Spout.

Trelaney and Spout cried out at the same time, Trelaney’s high-pitched call harmonizing with Spout’s husky grunt. In the cells all around, the captive wizards shivered with vicarious pleasure.

Still, he kept his orgasm at bay.

Spout toppled forward, spent, her elbows on Peter's chest. Trelaney detached herself from him with *schhhhloop!* and leaned forward, her small pink-nippled breasts brushing his shoulder. The two women kissed, briefly. Peter's cock, still inside Spout, nearly surged.

"I think he's nearly ready," whispered Trelaney, brushing back a string of hair plastered to Peter's face.

Spout pushed Peter deep inside of her one last time, then detached as well. "It's time, baby."

Both of the teachers slithered down Peter's fuzzy body. Trelaney gently flattened his puff of pubic hair to give Spout full access to his wood-hard shaft. She let the tip of her tongue dance up and down the full length, making him twitch with pleasure.

Trelaney shoved Spout out of the way and fully took his cock in her mouth.

"Mmm," moaned Peter.

Spout picked up one of the dildos from the bag on the floor and began to pleasure herself.

"Mmm," moaned several of the guys in the cells.

As Trelaney sucked hard, the tip of Peter's penis ballooned, purple, ready to explode.

As she worked her pussy with one hand, Spout grabbed the shaggy mop of Peter's hair and pulled him forward, kissing him deeply. He became doubly pleasured: one soft mouth working his own lips, one soft mouth working his penis-rod.

One fuzzy mouth working his ass.

Wait, what?

Peter separated from Spout to take a glance behind him. Somehow, his teddy bear was there. Its face was buried in his ass. A small, velvety bear tongue wriggled in and around his butt-hole. He'd never really considered butt stuff, but it felt nice.

Trelaney and Spout took a moment to glance at the bear, raised their eyebrows at each other, then turned their attention back to Peter.

Spout took a vibrator in her other hand and used it on Trelaney, who got back to sucking Peter's rapidly expanding penis. She moaned as she did, producing a pleasant buzz that complimented the fuzziness behind him like a fine wine complimenting a strong cheese. Completing the ensemble, Spout leaned forward to kiss him again, both her hands busy pleasuring herself and Trelaney.

Peter's penis became huge. He was tumbling over the edge, almost ready to come.

Trelaney reached for the water jug beside the bed and pulled back, but continued to jack Peter off as his entire body shook with pleasure.

"Oh God, now! Come for me, Peter!" shouted Trelaney as she shook too, clenching around the vibrator.

"Yes, yes!" shouted Spout as she came, wetness gushing around the dildo.

"Hrrrngh!!!" gushed Peter as a thick stream of jizz poured into the jug.

"Oooh *fuck* yeah!" yelled the teddy bear as a shower of white fluff flew into the air.

They all moaned in harmony as they shared their explosive orgasm.

But then Peter's pleasured turned to pain, because there was an actual literal explosion.

***

Peter brushed bits of rubble out of his chest hair. He coughed. Chunks of stone were raining down around him, though the dungeon had stopped shaking.

Trelaney lay unconscious beside the bed, and Spout was beside her trying to revive her. Peter stood up, surprised to find himself free. The chains around his hands and feet had disappeared as soon as the witches had gotten distracted by the crumbling building.

The locks on the surrounding cells had also popped open. Guys slowly pushed open the barred doors, reluctantly poking their heads out, as if they didn't really want to escape. Probably because they didn't really want to escape.

Mathieu was among them.

"Mathieu!" shouted Peter, because he was confused and needed to talk to somebody he recognized.

"Peter! Are you okay? What happened?"

"I have no idea. I've been confused this entire time, to be honest. What is even going on down here?"

Mathieu rolled his eyes. "Don't you see? They need our sperms, Peter."

"But why?"

"They're not real wizards, Peter! They're Guzzles!"

Guzzles. Rod had mentioned the word before; they were non-wizards that stole magic from real wizards. Peter's guts seemed to do a loop or something. It felt bad and scary but also good. If none of the teachers were real wizards, then Peter really wasn't so different after all.

"So why the sexual relations with students?" asked Peter.

"Gawd, Peter, you don't get it. They drink the jizzum of real wizards to absorb their power. They brought all of us magical folk here just to take our mystical semen."

Ms. Spout reached for the bucket beside her—the one sloshing with Peter's sperm. She tipped it upside down, drinking the come, letting it pour down her chin and onto her tattooed breasts, still exposed. Shit, she'd realize he wasn't a real wizard when his sperm wasn't magical.

Another explosion rumbled the room. The sound came from above.

"So who's attacking us?" asked Peter.

Mathieu's gaze flicked up. "That, I don't know. Maybe somebody has come to save us. All I know is that, if we're going to get out of this alive, there is only one thing we need to do—"

A stone fell on Mathieu.

"Mathieu?" asked Peter, but Mathieu did not answer, because most of his head was caved in and his brains were sliding down his shoulder.

Spout pulled Peter away as Mathieu collapsed. She had found a bath robe, and she slipped another one over his shoulders. Her chin was still wet with spunk.

"Come with me if you want to live," she said, winking as she said *come*. "We'll get out of this, Peter. We can fly away, just you and me.

Hand-in-hand, they headed upstairs, towards the explosions.

EIGHT

The mansion was in rough shape. The main doors had been replaced with a gaping hole. The hole gaped so hard that it allowed strange people to try forcing their way in. The school's teachers fought to keep that from happening.

Madame Olorin took a sip from a flask in her robe pocket and aimed a wand at a man in a silk kimono climbing through the impromptu doorway.

"Stop or I'll shoot!" screamed Madame Olorin.

The man in the kimono charged forward. His eyes glowed. His hands crackled with blue lightning energy electricity.

Madame Olorin shot a glob of magic from the tip of her wand. It hit the man in the chest, who went flying back out the door.

There was no sign of Maggie, or Rod. Rod was an asshole, who probably didn't even listen when Peter told him where he was going. Yet Peter found himself worrying for his roommate's safety nonetheless.

Spout led Peter through the basement doorway and around the edge of the room, trying to avoid the streaks of magical energy shooting back and forth between the attackers and the teachers, exploding as they hit the walls, sending clouds of dust and rubble into the air around them.

"I just have one question," said Peter.

"Go for it," said Spout.

"Where did my teddy bear come from and why was it eating my ass?"

Spout giggled as she scampered up the stairway, Peter close behind. "Magic, Peter! It doesn't always make sense. Sometimes when I'm lost in ecstasy, the magic gives me things I didn't even know I wanted. Deeply buried desires."

He remembered spending long, boring nights sitting on his teddy bear while he jacked off in the sub-basement of his aunt and uncle's home. Spout must have read his mind to conjure the teddy bear. "Oh, okay," he said.

He reached the top of the stairs and turned to survey the foyer below. A few students ran from the basement, climbing through the hole to freedom. Peter wondered if he should follow them.

His teddy bear emerged from the basement next, leading a dazed Mrs. Trelaney behind it. A beam of electricity shot from the gaping doorway and barely missed the teddy bear, blackening a piece of its ear.

"Mother*fucker*!" screamed the teddy bear. It charged. The man in the kimono surged forward, trying to gain ground and enter the mansion, but the teddy bear leapt and latched onto his face.

"You like this?" the teddy bear said as the man tried to tear it off his face. "You *like* this?" the teddy bear said, grinding its hips against the man's face, suffocating him.

Trelaney and other teachers pushed forward, determined to drive the attackers away. Peter couldn't see Maggie anywhere.

"Come on!" said Spout, grabbing Peter's hand.

"Where are we going?"

"The front door is now a gaping hole, so we're going to have to find another way out. Let's find a broom and fly away from here. You and me, Peter, forever."

"Hmm, okay," said Peter.

Spout led him down the upper hallways of the mansion, opening doors along the way. "There's gotta be a broom closet somewhere," she said. "Although, come to think of it, I've never seen Hardrod cleaning this dump like he's supposed to. That creep is always in the woods with his phone doing who-knows-what."

After Spout opened one of the doors along the hallway, a yelp issued from it. Peter peeked his head inside. His Quackenbushery teacher was frantically sucking off a confused-looking student. "Sorry," said Peter as he closed the door.

Magical sperm. It seemed pretty ridiculous.

They climbed to the third floor. Spout seemed to vibrate with enthusiasm. Her eyes were wild, not focusing on anything. Peter's sperm wasn't magical, but she was certainly acting as if it were, deluding herself. Would she even be able to fly away? If Guzzles had no magical power without drinking the spunk of wizards, the two of them could be in for a long fall into the ocean if they leapt out of a window with a broom.

"Listen," said Peter. Spout opened another door, desperately looking for a broom, ignoring him. "Listen! There's something I gotta tell you. I know all the students here are supposed to be magic, but there's been some kind of mistake. I'm actually not a—"

A door further down the hall flung open. Maggie swished out of her room, her mane of silky red hair floating around her.

"What are you doing, Pamela?" asked Maggie.

Spout sighed. "I'm getting Peter to safety."

"There's a battle going on downstairs. The best way to keep the students safe is to win it. You're not trying to escape and steal little Peter, are you?"

Spout stepped in front of Peter. "He's mine. We have something special together."

Maggie rolled her eyes. "You and Trelaney have been sampling the product again, haven't you?"

Spout's jaw clenched. Her hand lowered to the wand in her belt.

"Don't," said Maggie, the confidence in her husky voice chilling.

"I love you, Peter," said Spout as she grabbed her wand. Before she could even raise it, a loud bang filled the air; Maggie had her own wand raised in front of her, a curl of smoke rising from the tip.

Spout fell to the ground with a charred hole in the centre of her forehead.

"Shiiit," muttered Peter.

"Don't tell me you bought that love nonsense, Peter."

Peter wasn't sure what he felt. He was pretty confused, and kinda guilty, because Spout thought she'd gained Peter's magic, but she was deluded, and couldn't defend herself, and maybe she was dead because of it. He shrugged his shoulders.

"I'll show you something," said Maggie. "Come into my room."

Peter stepped into Maggie's room. The door slammed itself shut behind him, and a hundred tiny chains appeared out of nowhere to seal it shut.

***

"WTF?" asked Peter.

"I might need a hostage. Hope you don't mind," said Maggie. She pulled a curtain back from her window to peek outside. Shadows zipped past. Explosions and screams continued to echo from the lower floor.

"A hostage? Why? Why me?"

"You must know that you're special. I don't go sucking the peters of every Tom, Dick and Harry around here."

Peter smirked. "I know what's going on here. I know you're all Guzzles. You don't have to pretend it was only for fun."

Maggie sat on the bed, which was surrounded by empty jugs that had presumably held sperms. The corner of her mouth twitched. "You know our secret, do you?"

He sat beside her. "Yes. And I guess you know mine."

"All I know is that—"

"I'm not a real wizard," he said, and it felt positively orgasmic to blurt it out, finally admitting it to somebody other than Rod.

Maggie titled her head back and laughed. "Who told you that you're not a real wizard?"

"Um, nobody. I just … I've never done wizard things like all these other guys. Before coming here, my greatest accomplishment was getting 3000 retweets when I posted a picture of a turd shaped like Vin Diesel."

"Peter!" said Maggie through choking laughter. She was even prettier when she smiled. "Do you think we'd drag you here if you weren't a real wizard?"

"Must've been a mistake."

"Peter, your ejaculate was the most magical I've ever felt. Your magi-spermian count is through the roof. After I swallowed your come, I was casting cantrips all night, and I still had plenty left to go the next day." She gestured at the empty jugs around her. "I must have swallowed five guys' bull gravy just now, and I still don't feel as powerful as I did after our night together."

Peter gasped. "So you're telling me that I'm a … I'm actually, really—"

"You're a wizard, Peter."

He leaned over and kissed her. She stiffened with surprise for a moment, then opened her soft lips, letting her tongue dance around inside his mouth.

She leaned back. "We don't have much time. I want you to fuck me. It needs to be fast, and it needs to be hard."

Peter had never felt so powerful. He leapt onto Maggie, tearing away her purple robe as their faces smooshed together. Her pink nipples sprung free. Her patch of red pubic hair shone like fire.

Tearing away his own bath robes, Peter let his penis flop out. Even at half-mast, it was bigger than ever in anticipation of Maggie's touch. When she reached for it, it sprung to life like a shark in a tornado.

"Now," commanded Maggie, leaning back and letting her finger trace his dick for a moment before letting go. She spread her legs. Her lady-folds opened, surrounded by fiery and feathery hair, like a fleshy phoenix. Except it was Peter who felt like he was being reborn. Except the opposite of being born, because instead of something coming out, it was something going in.

It was his penis going in.

The tip entered first, twitching in response to her considerable wetness. The shaft entered next, clasped tightly by her warmth, wriggling and twisting around him.

"Mmm, yes, fill me up."

"You like my peter?" asked Peter.

"I like your peter."

"Yeah. Yeah, take my little peter," said Peter.

He made love to her slowly, feeling her perky breasts pushing at the puff of hair on his chest.

"Faster. We don't have much time," Maggie said, her husky voice commanding and irresistible. He fucked her faster, vibrating with pleasure. Becoming lost in it, he closed his eyes and his mind cleared. He forgot about all the danger around him. Forgot about wizards and Guzzles and magic. Her love-muffin felt so good that the feeling of the air around them—even of the bed underneath—baked away, and the only sensation was Maggie.

When he opened his eyes, the bed was at least 0.5 meters below. They were weightless, somehow supported only by each other. Yet Peter wasn't scared. He plunged into her with renewed gusto, and she writhed against him in rhythm.

He was close to coming, and some far-off portion of his brain wondered if his sperm would have a magical effect on Maggie if administered vaginally, or if it only worked orally.

She clenched up and dug her long nails into Peter's back. Pulled closer, he could smell her hair, cinnamonny and roselike. He was one thrust away from filling her up, when—

The side of Maggie's room pulled away, compressing into a single point before disappearing, like the whole wall was suddenly sucked down an invisible drain. Peter felt himself sucked along with it, his dick leaving Maggie with a *schlip!* just as both of them were about to explode with pleasure together.

As he tumbled head over heels out of the room and into the open air, he saw the cliff the mansion was perched on below, and below that, the roiling ocean. As he flipped and fell, he saw Maggie above; she had managed to keep from being sucked out of the room. She grabbed a wand and shot a beam of red energy from its tip. Following the beam to the other end, Peter saw who was responsible for sucking him from the mansion.

It was quite surprising who was responsible; someone who Peter had not expected.

The unexpected saboteur shot a beam of energy back at Maggie. The two beams sparked and crackled as they met in the middle.

As he fell, probably to his death, Peter again contemplated how much of a twist it was that the person responsible was who it was.

It was Hardrod.

NINE

As he fell to his death, Peter thought about Maggie, and her soft breasts bouncing against his chest.

Instead of splattering onto the rocky cliffs, his fall slowed. He felt warmth all around him. Fleshy warmth.

Balloons surrounded Peter. Conjured out of nowhere, the flesh-colored globes puffed into existence around him just before he hit the ground. They formed a soft platform, where he bounced once before they nudged him upright and eased him to the rocky surface.

Upon second look, they weren't balloons at all, but disembodied breasts, nipples and all. As quickly as they had appeared, they disappeared, doing that same thing the wall above had done and stretching into a funnel like they were going down a drain. Except the funnel ended at Peter's dick, still hard from his tryst with Maggie.

He heard Rod's words from when they were riding brooms on the Quiddix field.

A wand is anything that's long and hard.

Jacking himself off to stay hard, Peter closed his eyes and concentrated. "I really wish I had some clothing right now," he muttered as a mist from the ocean made him shiver.

His dick tingled for a moment, and he felt as if he were wetting himself. But when he opened his eyes, he was wearing his bath robe.

"Nice," he said.

The rocky platform beside the ocean was perfectly flat, as if it had been carved into the side of the cliff. Sure enough, there was a wooden door in the rocks, with some barrels beside that. Peter approached them and peered inside. The barrels were full of rings, gem stones, and coins.

The door burst open. Peter was nearly knocked over by Grand Wizard Felch, who was huffing and puffing.

"What the fuck are you doing here?" asked Felch.

Peter stammered. “I—I just—the attack—it was Hardrod—and I fell—and,”

"Shut up and get out of my way." Felch sighed and shoved Peter aside. He dug through one of the barrels and found a Rolex watch, then approached the edge of the cliff, facing the ocean.

"Hey!" he shouted. "Shiny. Shiiiny."

"What is going on?" asked Peter, regaining his composure.

Felch sneered. "Shut up. You didn't see this. You ... you can't see this. You've already seen too much." He reached for the wand looped in his belt string.

“Man, I just want to get out of here," said Peter.

"I almost had it all," said Felch, frowning. "My own magic was so powerful, but it wasn't enough. The other wizards wouldn't help me. I had to enlist the help of all these Guzzles." He spat, as if disgusted by saying the word.

“Dude, I never asked about any of this,” said Peter.

Felch continued as if he hadn’t heard. “The magic finally got its attention. My master. The old one from the deep below the deep.” He smiled, looking out at the ocean. “It is out there now. I can feel its presence. But its ancient power is secret, it has always been secret, and it needs to remain secret.”

Peter gulped: a reaction to being scared.

Felch reached for his wand. “Whoever you are, I’m sorry you had to come here. It’s part of something larger, you see. Something bigger than us all. I’m sorry you had to see this, and I’m sorry you have to die.”

He aimed the wand at Peter, who was unarmed, his penis flaccid with fear. He stepped back towards the water, his hands in the air.

Felch's wand glowed an angry purple.

As the wand shot a burst of energy aimed to kill Peter, a commotion arose behind him. Peter turned to see Rod leaping off of a ratty flying broom. He bowled into Peter as a fiery, electricity-ish ball of plasma soared overhead.

"Leave my friend alone!" shouted Rod, standing and raising a spoon.

"Thanks for saving me," whispered Peter.

"You told me you were coming down here to investigate. And I told you I'd be here for you, didn't I?"

"You did. Good job with the flying, by the dubs."

"Apparently almost dying really brings out the wizardry," said Rod, aiming his spoon at Felch, who still hadn't shot them while they had this conversation, for some reason.

Rod's spoon glowed white. Felch's wand glowed purple. They fired at the same time. Felch was unnaturally fast, dodging the blast of energy. Rod was less fast; the purple blast hit his hand, tearing it off, splattering Peter with blood.

"My hand tore off!" screamed Rod, waving around a stump that continued to spray blood all over as he fell to the ground.

"Dang," said Peter. He looked at Felch, who had hit the ground and lost grip of his wand. He looked at Rod, who had risked his life to save Peter despite their quarrelling.

He knew what to do.

Unstrapping his robe, he let his penis flop out. Using Rod's blood as lubricant, he furiously stroked himself. All the excitement of the past few days flashed through his mind: Maggie's lips in the bathroom, losing his virginity to Trelaney and Spout in the dungeon, then being with Maggie again, just a few minutes ago. Soon he was as long and hard as a tube of rock.

“Hey Rod,” he said. “Remember when I told you I wasn’t a real wizard?”

“Uh huh,” Rod said through sobs of pain.

“Well, guess what.” He aimed his massive dick at Felch. “I’m a motherfucking wizard.”

A many-coloured blast of globular energy shot from the tip of Peter’s penis. He cried out with pleasure, his body shaking in the most intense orgasm he had ever experienced. The energy hit Felch in the chest, knocking him back into the treasure barrels and leaving a red mist in the air.

He knelt beside Rod and concentrated on positive, healing thoughts, then slapped the wet tip of his penis against his friend’s stump. The bleeding stopped.

A groan sputtered from the corner. Felch was alive.

Peter got ready to stroke his flagging dick-wand back to full functionality, but then the ocean behind him seemed to explode, showering him with frigid water. He hunched over Rod, attempting to keep him safe. A shadow loomed over them.

It was a massive tentacle. Its olive skin was covered in light hair. An eye on a stalk peeked from over the edge of the cliff, guiding the tentacle over Peter and Rod to curl around Felch. As it picked him up, his heart flopped out of his chest and jiggled on the ground. He was dead now, probably.

“Get on!” shouted a deep voice to Peter’s side.

It was Hardrod, riding a polished mahogany broom. His eyes glowed blue with real magic.

Peter suddenly realized that Hardrod and the real wizards were good guys, and Felch and the Guzzles were bad guys. Besides, he had no other way out of there. He ducked under the tentacle as it retreated to the ocean, dragging Rod with him. His friend slumped onto Hardrod’s broom and wrapped his arms around the large man, to keep from falling. Peter got on behind him. Luckily, his boner had subsided.

As they flew away, a rumbling voice, so deep that Peter could hardly tell if he was hearing it or imagining it, said: "*SHINY*."

A small tentacle shot from the ocean and wrapped around the barrels full of treasure. From above, Peter saw the tentacles return to a tangle of eyes, pincers, beaks, and other monstrous bits, all peeking from the ocean, where the swelling of the water hinted at a much larger mass underneath the water.

"We'd best get out of here, boys," said Hardrod.

"You came to save us?" asked Peter.

"You bet. All the other guys are already loaded in vans. We're taking you to the real wizarding school."

The creature took a chunk of cliff with it as it slithered back into the water, causing the cave where Peter had been moments earlier to cave in, as caves do. The rest of the mansion had been relying on that cliff for support, so it began crumbling and tumbling into the ocean.

The other side of the mansion was crumbling too. Half of the mushroom-tipped columns had been obliterated by the attacking wizards. The Guzzle fired back, but it was futile. Maggie was down there, ducking behind a pile of rubble. She looked up at the sky, at Peter, sadness filling her violet eyes, before making a run for the forest.

Peter sighed as the broom carried them away. "Wait, if you were a real wizard all along, and were planning on rescuing us from the Guzzles, why did you help them collect all of us at the beginning of this story?"

Hardrod laughed deeply. "Magic, Peter! It doesn't always make sense!"

EPILOGUE

Dear Aunt and Uncle,

Things are good at the real wizarding school. I got here in a phallically-shaped train that went through like fifty tunnels. I don't know if you know this, but wizards seem to be obsessed with sexual imagery and activities.

Yeah, so, apparently I was a wizard my whole life and you never told me, which is kind of a dick move. Even when I reached the legal age of consent in our state, which is when wizards reach their full magical potential, you didn't think it would be worth mentioning? Surely my parents were wizards and told you about this at some point?

Lame.

Anyways, classes are going okay. It's hard to do magic when my life isn't in danger, but I'm learning. I can even do spells with a wand instead of my dick, sometimes.

The Guzzles who survived the attack on the mansion are out there and want revenge. Plus there's some giant evil monster out there in the ocean. So maybe my life will be in danger again soon. You probably don't care, but in case you don't hear from me, it's because I'm dead. Read the sequel to find out what happened.

I know you're afraid. You're afraid of us. You're afraid of change. But I'm going to put down this pen and return to a world without you, a world without rules and controls, without borders or boundaries, a world where anything is possible.

Fuck you. I'm a motherfucking wizard.

About Forest City Pulp

Forest City Pulp publishes provocative fiction by provocative writers. It was founded in 2012 to take full advantage of the digital reality of publishing, and is designed to evolve as quickly as technology does. Visit http://www.forestcitypulp.com or @ForestCityPulp for more information, and send us an electronic communication if you would like to get involved.

If you were amused by this book, please take a few minutes to **leave an honest review** wherever you got it and share it with whoever you hang out with, digitally or physically. We are tiny and want to grow organically, without marketing stunts or other douchebaggery. Every bit helps.

Sign up (http://eepurl.com/WZPvD) so we can let you know when Leonard has new stuff or FCP books are on sale.

Also by Leonard Delaney: Sex Boat

When Winston left for a tropical vacation on a boat, he did not expect to be alone. Yet here he is, on a boat, holding the diamond ring he intended to propose to Brooke with, while she's been held back by her job. Lame. But things start to perk up when a party girl with a dark side and a blue-eyed bombshell with an ocean obsession both express sexual feelings about him. Winston has some choices to make about how to spend his vacation. Meanwhile, a mysterious force from the depths of the ocean has other plans for the boat.

Erotic, exhilarating, sexual, exciting, and mysterious, Sex Boat is a caper that will wiggle its way inside of you and make you reluctant to remove it. Just wait until you see the alarming finale.

Made in the USA
Columbia, SC
14 December 2023

28547848R00038